I Was an
Outer-Space Chicken

To the students and staff at Turtle Lake Elementary,
I can always COUNT on you to MULTIPLY my smiles
and ADD joy to my day when I visit your school. —D.L.

To Steve, Jess, and Irene:
Thanks for all the opportunity and support over the past year.
It made a world of difference. —M.G.

STERLING CHILDREN'S BOOKS
New York

An Imprint of Sterling Publishing Co., Inc.
1166 Avenue of the Americas
New York, NY 10036

ISBN 978-1-4549-2921-5

Distributed in Canada by Sterling Publishing Co., Inc.
C/o Canadian Manda Group, 664 Annette Street
Toronto, Ontario M6S 2C8, Canada
Distributed in the United Kingdom by GMC Distribution Services
Castle Place, 166 High Street, Lewes, East Sussex BN7 1XU, England
Distributed in Australia by NewSouth Books
University of New South Wales, Sydney, NSW 2052, Australia

For information about custom editions, special sales, and premium and
corporate purchases, please contact Sterling Special Sales at 800-805-5489 or
specialsales@sterlingpublishing.com.

Manufactured in Canada

Lot #:
2 4 6 8 10 9 7 5 3 1
05/19

sterlingpublishing.com
Cover and interior design by Irene Vandervoort

ALIEN MATH

SERIES
Book Number One

I WAS AN Outer-Space Chicken

by DAVID LaROCHELLE
illustrated by MIKE GORMAN

STERLING CHILDREN'S BOOKS
New York

CHAPTER 1

Elevator to the Unknown

If you're going to be abducted by an alien, it helps to bring along a good friend, and Lamar Wilson is an *excellent* friend.

We were standing on the sidewalk in front of our apartment building. The school bus had just dropped us off and we were kicking a soccer ball back and forth between us.

"32 plus 16," said Lamar, and kicked the ball toward me.

"48!" I answered as I stopped the ball with the toe of my tennis shoe.

"100 minus 59," I said, then kicked the ball back to him.

"41!" answered Lamar, trapping the ball with his foot.

Lamar and I are co-captains of our school's Math All-Stars team, and we were practicing math problems in preparation for our first tournament of the year. Lamar and I live in the same apartment building and have known each other since preschool, which is 2,615 days. He is 37 days older than I am. He has one-fourth as many goldfish as I do (I have eight). He lives in apartment 503, which is the reverse number of my apartment, 305. And he also loves numbers just as much as I do.

"Okay, Lexie, here comes a tough one: 28 plus 2, minus 10, plus 49."

"Piece of cake," I said. "Sixty—"

SMASH!

The soccer ball bounced past me, hit the stoop, and crashed into Mrs. Kruegel's gigantic jar of sun tea that she always keeps sitting on the front steps. The glass jar shattered into approximately one hundred seventy-four pieces, splattering amber-colored tea in every direction.

"Uh-oh," I said. "I think we're in trouble."

Lamar frowned. "Not just trouble," he said. "BIG trouble."

BIG trouble because Mrs. Kruegel is the crabbiest woman in our building . . . and I have the facts to prove it:

1. She owns *three* vicious Chihuahuas.
2. She has *four* "Keep Quiet!" signs posted around the apartment.
3. She has called my father *five* different times to complain that I leave gum wrappers in the hallways.

I do NOT leave gum wrappers in the hallways. Ever.

Lamar picked up the soccer ball from the puddle of tea and wiped it off on his jeans. "Well, we might as well get this over with," he said. "C'mon." He walked up the steps into our apartment building's lobby.

That's one of the things that makes Lamar such a great co-captain. He's good at taking charge and making a plan of action. That's helpful when our math team is stuck on a problem and we can't agree on how to solve it. I, on the other hand, am good at noticing the details that other people sometimes overlook. Together we make a powerful pair.

We walked into the elevator, and Lamar pushed the button for the fourth floor. If you add my apartment number to Lamar's, then divide by 2, you get Mrs. Kruegel's number. It's an apartment I try to stay as far away from as possible.

"I'll ring her buzzer," Lamar said, "and then you can tell her what happened."

"Wait a minute!" I said. "How come I have to tell her what happened?"

"Because you're the one who missed the ball," he said.

"But you're the one who kicked it," I answered.

I've calculated that Lamar and I get along 91 percent of the time, which is pretty good if you ask me. But it looked like we were heading into that troublesome other 9 percent.

"There's nothing to worry about, Lexie. Mrs. Kruegel doesn't breathe fire," said Lamar.

I wasn't so sure about that.

"Then *you* tell her," I said. "Unless you're afraid."

"*I'm* not afraid," he said. "I'm ringing her doorbell. You're the one who's being a chicken."

"Me? *You're* the chicken!"

That's when the elevator was filled with a blinding flash of green light. The flash was followed by the crackling sound of a thousand fireworks going off at once. The air temperature jumped to a fiery 120 degrees, then plummeted to only a tenth of that.

The next thing I knew, Lamar and I were no longer in the elevator. We were sitting scrunched inside a small metal cage that wasn't much bigger than a dog kennel. Three inches away, on the outside of the metal bars, was a furry purple face. Two wiry antennae sprouted from the top of its head, each topped with an eye the size of a ping-pong ball. One eye swiveled to look at Lamar, the other eye swiveled to look at me. Then the face smiled, revealing a mouth filled with more razor-sharp teeth than legs on a pair of centipedes.

CHAPTER 12 ÷ 6

Outer-Space Chickens

I screamed. I think Lamar screamed too.

"Ah, do not be upset," said the creature. Its voice was high-pitched and squeaky, like the two rusty hinges on my grandpa's toolbox. "I know what will make you happy."

The furry face moved back. It was connected to a shaggy body that looked like a larger version of my Aunt Lillian's Yorkshire terrier, except that it had six feet and two tails. The creature reached into a circular metal bin with one of its feet and began throwing hard yellow pellets at us.

We raised our hands to protect our faces.

"Cut it out!" said Lamar.

"What is the matter?" said the creature. "Are you not hungry? I thought this was the food that chickens like to eat."

I looked at the floor of the cage. The little yellow pellets were dried kernels of corn.

"We're not chickens!" said Lamar.

The creature smiled again revealing its piranha teeth, each one a perfect equilateral triangle.

"Ah, you cannot fool me. Moments ago my ship's audio beam clearly heard the two of you refer to each other as chickens. I am on a mission to collect strange and unusual species for my planet's zoo and I was instructed to bring back two chickens from planet Earth. And here you are!"

"We are *not* chickens," I said. "When we called each other a chicken, we just meant that the other person was afraid."

The alien did not look convinced.

"Listen," said Lamar. "Do we *look* like chickens?"

"You look exactly like chickens," said the creature.

It pushed a square button on a glowing control panel and a giant six-foot by four-foot screen appeared. An image flashed onto the screen showing a kid our age holding a white fluffy chicken. Beneath the image were the words:

Earth file 3893K-5N: The Chicken
Eats "corn"
Produces round white objects called "eggs"
Intelligence level: Extremely Low

The alien pointed to the image of the kid. "See. You look very much like this chicken."

"That's not a chicken!" said Lamar. "That's a human being. The chicken is in the kid's hands."

The creature looked at the screen, then back at us, then back at the screen again. It padded up to our cage on all six legs and peered at us closely. I felt like a lab experiment being examined by a scientist. A furry, purple scientist.

"How do I know you are not trying to fool me?" it said.

"For one thing, we don't eat dried-up corn," said Lamar. "And for a second thing, we don't lay eggs."

"And for a third thing," I added, "our intelligence level is a *lot* higher than a chicken's."

The alien stared at us with its creepy antenna eyes for a full ninety seconds. Every time the right eye blinked, the left eye blinked twice. It was hypnotizing.

Finally the creature said, "Well . . . if you are truly smarter than a chicken, I do not want to make a mistake and return home with the wrong animal."

"Good!" I said, relieved I wasn't going to spend the rest of my life on display in some alien's zoo.

"So will you let us out of this cage?" said Lamar. "My legs are getting cramped."

The creature kept its eyes trained on us as it unlocked the cage. We crawled out and stretched.

"You have forgotten your egg," said the creature.

"It's not an egg," said Lamar, "it's my soccer ball." He reached inside the cage and picked up the ball. "Now if you don't mind, Mr. Alien, please take us home."

"I am not a *mister*," said the creature. "I am a female. And my name is Foozen-Allwyn-Crypto-Noomin-Regan-Zenar-Mush-Mush."

Wow. I thought *my* name was long: Alexis Elizabeth-Anne Wellington. She must have me beat by at least ten letters.

"But if that is too difficult for you chickens to pronounce . . ."

"We are human beings!" Lamar and I said.

". . . then you may call me Fooz," continued the alien.

"Nice to meet you, Fooz," I said. "My name is Lexie, this is Lamar, and we need to get back to Earth right away. My dad will go crazy if I'm not there when he gets home."

"And my parents are counting on me to pick up my little brother from the babysitter," said Lamar.

"And we'll both be late if we're not home in . . ." I checked my watch. "Thirty-seven minutes—give or take sixteen seconds."

"Yes, yes, right away," said Fooz. "But first, would the two of you chick—I mean human beings—help me with a small task? It is time to feed three of the other creatures I have collected during my travels. Their names are Fluffy, Puffy, and Muffy. You will find them at the back of the ship."

Fooz held up a clear cylinder filled with something that looked like fuzzy blue golf balls.

"These are bogberries," she said, "and it is the only food they will eat." She handed me the cylinder. "And this is *exactly* how much food they should be fed."

There were seven layers of berries in the tube, and five of the furry berries on each layer.

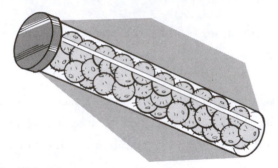

"I will begin programming the ship to take you back to Earth if you will feed Fluffy, Puffy, and Muffy . . . unless you think the task is too difficult for you."

"Don't worry," said Lamar. "We can handle it. We'll be done before you can count to 50 by 5s."

"One more thing," said Fooz, "and this is very important." Her voice grew low and deep. "Do NOT overfeed or underfeed them."

"No problem," said Lamar.

We left Fooz at her control panel and headed to the back of the ship, passing crates and jars filled with the oddest animals I've ever seen . . . and I mean *odd*: a nine-headed snake, a seven-legged lizard, and a three-horned turtle with five wings sprouting from its shell.

"The other kids on the math team are never going to believe this," I said. "I wonder where Fooz found all—"

I bumped into Lamar. He was staring at three large cages labeled Fluffy, Puffy, and Muffy. Inside each cage was a quivering eight-foot tower of goo that looked like it was made out of gray oatmeal. No eyes, no ears, just gigantic slobbery openings for their mouths. Inside the openings were pointy nail-like teeth that rotated around the mouths like the blades of a chainsaw.

"Ew," said Lamar. "They look like something that crawled out of a toxic waste dump."

"I'm glad we're on *this* side of the cages," I said.

Lamar reached into the tube and took out a bogberry. "Well, let's get them fed so we can go home."

He was about to toss the fuzzy berry into one of the cages when I grabbed his wrist.

"Wait!" I said, and pointed to a small sign at the bottom of the cages:

FEEDING INSTRUCTIONS

Fluffy eats twice as much as Puffy

Puffy eats twice as much as Muffy

"Hmmmm," said Lamar. "That makes this a *lot* more interesting."

And then I noticed something else.

"Take a look at Fooz," I whispered.

We glanced over our shoulders. Fooz had told us she was going to start programming the ship to take us back home, but instead she was staring at us with her ping-pong-ball eyes. When she caught us looking, she quickly swiveled her eyes in the other direction.

"What's up with her?" said Lamar.

I had a pretty good idea.

"I think Fooz still thinks we're chickens. I think she's

testing us to see if we're smart enough to figure out how much these blobs eat."

"A test?" said Lamar. His eyes lit up like the display on a calculator. A smile as wide as a protractor crept across his face. He got the same look of determination he always gets before one of our math tournaments. "Ha! We'll show her we're not chickens."

Lamar reread the feeding instructions out loud.

"*Fluffy eats twice as much as Puffy. Puffy eats twice as much as Muffy.*" He looked at the clear cylinder Fooz had given me and I could tell his brain was shifting into high gear. "We can handle this, Lexie. First things first: how many bogberries do we have?"

That was easy. I had calculated that the moment Fooz had given me the cylinder. Seven layers of berries, five berries on each layer...

"Thirty-five," I answered.

Then I noticed one more thing. The blobs were sending out long tentacles of gray goo that were oozing out from beneath their cages. The tentacles looked like hungry snakes in search of a snack . . . and they were heading straight for our feet. If my estimate was correct, they'd reach our shoes in slightly less than fifty-five seconds.

We needed to solve this problem *fast*. And if we didn't want Fooz to think that we were chickens, we needed to get the answer *right*.

CHAPTER (6 + 3) − (4 + 2)

Feeding Time

"Let's start with a good guess," said Lamar. "How many bogberries do you think we should feed Muffy?"

I didn't know the answer, but I made my best guesstimate.

"Seven."

"If we feed seven for Muffy, we need twice as many for Puffy, and twice that for Fluffy," said Lamar. "7 + 14 + 28 equals . . . 49. Nope. We don't have that many berries."

By now one of the tentacles of goo had nearly reached my left shoe. I inched backward a foot and a half.

"How about if we feed six berries to Muffy?" asked Lamar.

I did my best to ignore the gooey tentacle which was still creeping toward me and concentrated on the math.

"That's 6 + 12 + 24, which equals . . . 42," I said. "Still too much."

Then I gasped. Something wet had wrapped around my ankle. It was one of the gray tentacles oozing from Fluffy's cage. It tightened around my ankle and began slithering up my leg. I tried to shake it loose, but couldn't. I saw that Lamar was struggling to pull free from a tentacle that had grabbed his leg as well.

I shivered in disgust, but as gross as it was to be grabbed by this slimy creature, we had something more important to think about. We had a math problem to finish.

Lamar looked at me, I looked at him, and at the same moment we shouted, "Five!"

Five berries for Muffy, plus ten berries for Puffy, plus twenty berries for Fluffy: 5 + 10 + 20 totaled 35. That was the exact amount we needed to feed these three piles of goo.

"Quick!" said Lamar. "You feed Muffy, I'll feed Puffy, and the remaining berries will go to Fluffy!"

We began tossing the fuzzy berries into the slimy mouths, counting carefully as we did, which wasn't the easiest thing to do with ooze slithering up our bodies. As the berries landed in the mouths, they were chewed to bits by the chainsaw teeth. The grinding noise reminded me of the time I accidentally dropped a box of sixty metal paperclips down our garbage disposal.

We finished feeding Muffy and Puffy and threw the last twenty berries into Fluffy's gaping mouth.

The goo kept worming up our legs.

Had we made a mistake with the math? Had we miscounted the berries we had fed them? I was positive we hadn't.

Then slowly the teeth stopped rotating. The slimy tentacles loosened their grip. As they seeped back into their cages, I shook myself hard, glad to be free of the goop.

"Way to go!" said Lamar, and we gave each other our math team's victory cheer, a triple high five.

"It looks like you are not chickens after all."

We turned around. Fooz was standing right behind us.

"That's what we've been trying to tell you!" said Lamar.

"So will you take us home now?" I asked.

"Yes, yes," said Fooz. "Of course, definitely, right away. Except . . ."

"Except what?"

"Except I am running low on fuel and I need to make a stop at a nearby planet to refill my fuel pods."

"This isn't another test to check whether we're chickens?" I asked.

"No, no. Absolutely not."

"How long will that take?" asked Lamar.

"It will not take long at all," said Fooz. "I have six fuel pods and each one requires only fifteen minutes to fill."

"That's ninety minutes!" I said.

"An hour and a half!" said Lamar.

"Five thousand four hundred seconds!" we both said at the same time.

My dad was going to be furious when I came home

so late. I'd be grounded for the rest of my life. Assuming I lived to be one hundred, that was eighty-nine years of punishment!

But we didn't have much choice. It wasn't like we could take a taxi or bus to get back home.

Fooz told us to strap ourselves in for the landing. We found a pair of seats wedged between two stacks of cages. We had just lowered the shoulder harnesses over our heads when the ship began to shake and rattle so hard I was afraid the cages would crash down on top of us. To calm myself, I did what I always do when I'm worried. I counted.

I counted the animals in the cages to my left: 21.

I counted the animals in the cages to my right: 38.

I counted the animals in the cages hanging from the ceiling, which was more than the number of animals to my left, less than the number of animals to my right, and an even-numbered multiple of 5.

I had just started counting the number of squawks from a two-headed parrot when the spaceship gave an especially large bounce and . . . stopped.

"Welcome to planet Flacknar!" said Fooz.

We scrambled to the front of the ship and looked out the enormous elliptical window. We had landed alongside something that looked like an inky black lake.

"What's that?" I asked.

"A pool of fludge," said Fooz.

"It looks like tar," said Lamar, "or chocolate sauce. Is that what your ship uses for fuel?"

"My ship can convert any liquid to fuel," said Fooz.

"On Flacknar, fludge is considered liquid garbage. They will be happy for its removal." She opened a hatch on the floor. "I am going to head down to the fuel bay and send out a collection hose."

Lamar was still looking out the window.

"Fooz, while you're collecting fludge, do you think Lexie and I could go outside and take a look around?"

Fooz glanced at her control panel. "The air is compatible to the atmosphere of Earth. It should be perfectly safe for the two of you to step outside."

Remembering our encounter with Muffy, Puffy, and Fluffy, I asked, "Are there any dangerous creatures on this planet? Creatures that would want to eat Earthlings like us?"

"Oh, no. Definitely not. All of the inhabitants of Flacknar are perfectly harmless. Except perhaps for Lumfurs, but they are rare. I do not think you will encounter one. A very unusual creature. You grab its long curly tail, and it will fall asleep immediately."

That didn't seem too dangerous. And who knows when I'd get the chance to visit another planet again? This wasn't an opportunity I wanted to miss.

Fooz tapped a button on her control panel three times and a triangular door appeared in the side of the ship. If she had tapped it six times, I wondered if a hexagonal door would have appeared. Before I could ask her, Lamar began heading down the ramp that led to the ground outside. I wasn't going to let him explore this planet without me, so I hurried to catch up.

The first thing I noticed were the colors. It looked like someone had taken a rainbow and multiplied the colors by ten thousand. The sky was a blazing yellow, the ground was a neon orange, and there were hundreds of deep magenta bushes the size of delivery trucks, each bursting with flowers in shades I had never even seen before. The intensity was so bright, my eyes began to water.

Then I noticed the heat. It was as hot and sticky as a ninety-eight-degree day in July with a humidity of 83 percent. I hadn't been out of the spaceship for more than a minute and already three-inch trickles of sweat were dripping down my back.

And then I noticed the strangest tree I had ever seen in my life. Its trunk was as straight and round as a telephone pole. I tried to see its top, but it seemed to stretch to infinity. Its skinny branches stuck out perpendicular from the trunk at precise ninety-degree angles.

The first branch had only one red leaf, perfectly shaped like a square. The second branch had four square-shaped leaves. The third branch had nine leaves. And the fourth branch had . . . sixteen leaves.

Hmm.

I made a prediction. And I was right. The fifth branch had twenty-five leaves.

"Hey, Lamar!" I called. He was about seven yards away, watching a pair of pink frog-like animals jump back and forth across themselves. "How many leaves do you think are on the tenth branch of this tree?"

Lamar shaded his eyes and looked up into the branches.

"Beats me." Then his eyes narrowed as he looked at the lower branches. I could tell he was studying them and counting.

He smiled.

"One hundred," he said. "Exactly one hundred. You can't stump me, Lexie!"

I grinned back. He had figured out the pattern as quickly as I had. If everything on Flacknar was as orderly as this tree, I was going to like this planet.

"If you think that's cool," said Lamar, "come over here and take a look at these—"

That's when a huge shaggy creature that looked like a cross between my Uncle Melvin and Bigfoot stepped out from behind a bush.

WHUMP!

He tossed a bag over Lamar's body.

THUMP!

He swung Lamar over his shoulder.

And *BUMP! BUMP! BUMP!*

He began walking away, with Lamar bouncing on his back.

My first thought was to run and get Fooz, but she was down in the fuel bay. It would take me a minute and a half to run and get her and another minute and a half to bring her back. In three minutes, Lamar would be long gone.

As the creature loped away through the bushes, I noticed his curly ropelike tail bouncing behind him. Was this a Lumfur? If it was, Fooz had said that grabbing its tail would put the creature to sleep.

I didn't have a nanosecond to waste. I started running to catch up with the Lumfur, but I had taken only four steps when—

WHUMP!

Something came down over my head.

THUMP!

I was lifted into the air and swung upside down.

And *BUMP! BUMP! BUMP!*

In less time than it takes to count the sides of an octagon, I was being carried off, just like Lamar.

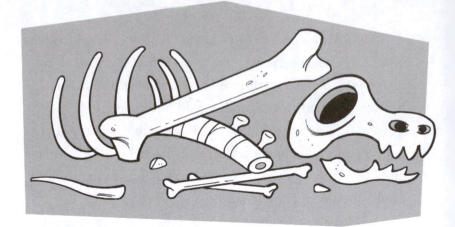

CHAPTER IV

Dinner Time

The inside of the Lumfur's bag smelled awful. It was a mixture of 64 percent burnt rubber, 27 percent sweaty gym socks, and 8 percent dead skunk. The remaining 1 percent smelled like dirty diapers.

If I thought it was warm before, it was even hotter inside the stuffy bag. I tried to wiggle around to find an opening where I could poke my nose out to get some fresh air. The bag, however, was too tight, and I couldn't wiggle more than a decimeter.

It would have been easy to panic, but I've learned from all my math tournaments that panicking doesn't solve a problem. So once again I returned to my favorite way to keep calm: counting. There wasn't much to count inside the bag other than the number of times I bounced against the Lumfur's back, so that's what I did:

1, 2, 3, 4 . . .

. . . 597, 598, 599 . . .

I had just reached the largest even number less than 2,000 made of all different digits when—

"*Ooof!*"

I was dumped out of the sack.

For the second time that day I found myself surrounded by the metal bars of a cage. Thankfully this cage was big enough for me to stand up in. As I got to my feet, the Lumfur slammed the door shut and growled at me like a broken lawnmower. Then he spat a slimy purple glob onto the ground and strode into the bushes with his empty sack swung over his shoulder.

"This planet needs a friendlier welcoming committee," said Lamar. He was standing in another cage, twenty-five feet away.

"You can say that again," I said.

I pushed on the cage door with all my weight (76 and ¾ pounds), but the door was locked tight. I wasn't surprised.

"The bars of the cage don't bend either," said Lamar. "I've tried."

I took three deep breaths, trying to clear my nose from the stench of the Lumfur's sack. Then I took a good look at my surroundings.

I was standing in a circle of cages. A dozen to be exact. Lamar was in the cage directly opposite mine. All of the cages were numbered consecutively, like the hours on the face of a clock. The number on Lamar's cage said 11, and even though I couldn't see the front of my cage, it was easy to figure out which number it was.

29

The rest of the cages were empty. The area in the center of the circle was bare, except for a lot of white sticks scattered on the ground. I estimated more than 160 but less than 220. Some of the sticks were as small as pencil stubs and some were as long as rulers. I knelt on the bottom of the cage and squeezed my arm between two of the bars so I could grab one for a closer look.

It wasn't a stick at all. It was a bone. A bone that had been gnawed clean by very sharp teeth.

Just then another Lumfur appeared. He had two sacks swung over his shoulder. He stopped in front of cage 1. With his free hand he grabbed a silver box that was hanging from a cord around his neck. The box looked like a TV remote. He pointed the remote at the front of the cage and pushed buttons with his rubbery thumb.

"Two, zero, two," he growled.

Pop! The door of the cage swung open.

The Lumfur shook one of the bags and out tumbled a trembling creature that looked like a lime-green rabbit with three ears. The rabbit scrambled to the back of the cage and cowered as the Lumfur slammed the cage door shut.

Then he walked over to cage 3. This time he growled, "Four, two, six," as he pushed buttons on the remote.

Pop! The door of that cage opened and the Lumfur emptied a yellow rabbit out of a sack before slamming the door shut.

"Hey!" called Lamar. "If you don't mind, would you let us out? We don't want to miss our ride back home."

The Lumfur's bloodshot eyes tripled in size. He bent

down, scooped up one of the bones, and threw it hard at Lamar.

The bone spun through the air, then—*CLONK!*—bounced off the metal bars of Lamar's cage and landed on the spongy orange ground with a thud.

"Rawwwwwwrrr!" snarled the Lumfur. With an angry look over his shoulder, he disappeared into the bushes.

"Sheesh!" said Lamar. "And I thought my older brother was a grump."

"We've got to get out of here," I told Lamar. I tossed the bone I was holding as far from my cage as I could. "We don't want to be around when these creatures start to get hungry."

"You've got that right," he said, "and I have a plan. We've got to get our hands on one of those remotes. They're the key to opening these cages. If we can lure one of those Lumfurs close enough, we can grab his tail and put him to sleep, then take his remote."

Like most of Lamar's plans, this was a good one. Except one thing bothered me. Even if we got our hands on one of the remotes, we didn't know how they worked.

The numbers 2, 0, 2 had opened up cage 1. The numbers 4, 2, 6 had opened cage 3. But were these random codes? If they were, we were sunk. We could spend days punching in numbers hoping to find the right combinations to open our locked doors.

On the other hand . . . if the codes were a pattern, then maybe we had a chance of figuring out how they worked.

Just then another Lumfur appeared. I watched him carefully as he stopped at a cage three spots to my left. He held out the remote and pushed buttons as he growled, "Nine, seven, sixteen." The door popped open, and he flung a frightened rabbit inside. A yellow rabbit again.

Lamar had been watching the Lumfur as well. He waited until the creature was passing his cage, then thrust his hand through the bars to grab his tail. The hairy tail swished to the side a fraction of an inch, just as Lamar reached out his arm. He missed. Without noticing, the Lumfur kept walking and was gone again.

"Rats!" said Lamar. "But I'll get him next time."

While Lamar puzzled over ways to lure the Lumfur closer, I thought about the numbers that the Lumfurs had used to open the three different cages. Something in my gut insisted that they weren't random, but what was the pattern?

I was about to ask Lamar if he had any ideas when I came up with an idea of my own. Perhaps the codes that opened the doors were related to the cage numbers. One by one I compared each cage number to the code that had opened it and tried to find a connection.

Slowly things began to fall into place, and then . . .

Bingo! The pattern was clear!

Well . . . I was pretty sure I had figured out the pattern, but I wanted one more example to confirm my theory.

"GROARRRRRR!"

That's when another Lumfur stepped out from an opening in the bushes. He looked even grumpier than the others if that was possible. I noticed right away that this one wasn't carrying a sack.

Starting with cage 1 he began walking clockwise around the circle, stopping at the occupied cages and sniffing.

When the Lumfur reached my cage he stopped and sniffed a long time. As he sniffed, he drooled. Enough drool to fill two and a half measuring cups. Then he smiled and licked his lips.

The Lumfur grabbed the remote that was hanging around his neck. He pointed it at the numbered sign in front of my cage, pushing buttons, and growling, "Six, four, ten."

The door to my cage swung open.

The Lumfur stepped inside.

Half of me was terrified, the way I feel in a nightmare when I discover I haven't turned in any of my math assignments all trimester.

But the other half of me felt triumphant. The numbers that the Lumfur had used to open my cage matched the pattern I had predicted. I knew how the remote control boxes worked!

Unfortunately my brain breakthrough wasn't going to do me much good. The Lumfur was facing me head on. There was no way I could reach around his massive body to grab his tail so I could put him to sleep. Lamar couldn't help me either; he was locked in a cage twenty-five feet away.

The Lumfur took a step closer. I could see that his fur was crawling with tiny bugs the size of decimal points. Then he reached out his arm, pointed a fat finger at me, and roared a single word:

"DINNER!"

CHAPTER 1 ½ + 3 ½

Which Way, Lincoln?

I inched myself into a corner of my cage.

"Wouldn't you rather have a salad instead?" I told the Lumfur. "A big strong guy like you needs at least three cups of vegetables a day. Yum! Doesn't a nice crunchy carrot sound tasty?"

"Tasty!" he repeated, looking at me and patting his stomach. He took another step closer and, before I could count the warts on his nose, the Lumfur grabbed me with both of his hands, pinning my arms to my sides. He lifted me off the ground and into the air. I ducked my head so it wouldn't scrape the top of the cage.

Was this the end? Would I never win another medal at the Math All-Stars?

Not if I could help it.

I swung my leg back and kicked the Lumfur with my

size 4 tennis shoe. I may be small, but I've got a dynamite kick, thanks to all the years of playing soccer with Lamar. But despite six well-aimed kicks to his belly, the Lumfur didn't even flinch. His gut must have been made of ¾-inch concrete. All he did was squeeze me tighter.

Whiff!

Something whizzed through the air on the left side of the cage.

Whiff!

Something whizzed through the air on the right side of the cage.

"Hey! Leave her alone, you big hairball!"

It was Lamar. He was throwing bones at the Lumfur from his locked cage on the other side of the circle.

The Lumfur didn't even swivel his head, but kept his hungry eyes focused straight at me. As his grip tightened, my ribs felt ready to snap like pretzel sticks.

"I said leave her alone, NOW!"

BONK!

One of the bones that Lamar was throwing sailed through the door of the cage and hit the Lumfur in the back of his shaggy head.

"ROOOOOOWWWWWGL!"

That got his attention. If the first Lumfur had sounded like a lawnmower, this one sounded like a Boeing 747 on takeoff.

The Lumfur dropped me to the ground. Clutching his head with his two giant hands, he spun around to see what had hit him.

I didn't let this chance escape. As soon as his back was toward me, I grabbed the Lumfur's hairy tail with both of my hands and . . .

THUNK!

Just like that, he collapsed into a furry heap on the floor of the cage. Five seconds later, the softest, gentlest snore came whispering from the Lumfur's blubbery lips, sounding like a quintet of tiny kittens purring. To be sure he was really asleep, I held my breath and counted. Twenty-five snores later, he still hadn't moved a muscle.

I looked across the circle to Lamar who had a satisfied grin on his face. I was about to shout back my appreciation, but then I looked at the sleeping Lumfur and decided to be quiet. Carefully I stepped over his massive body. I didn't want to touch his smelly, bug-infested fur, but we needed his remote. Trying not to breathe through my nose, I bent down close to his neck and found a clasp on the cord. When I opened the clasp, the cord and the remote slipped easily off his neck.

As quietly as I could, I pushed the cage door shut, locking the sleeping Lumfur inside. Then I hurried over to Lamar. Now that I was sure of the pattern, opening his cage would be easy.

I pointed the remote at the number 11 on the front of Lamar's cage.

"One *more* than your cage number," I said, and pushed the button for 12.

"One *less* than your cage number," I said, and pushed the button for 10.

"And *double* your cage number," I said, and pushed the button for 22.

The door to his cage popped open and Lamar hopped out.

"Sweet!" he said. "Thanks for getting me out of there, Lexie."

"Thanks for saving me from becoming that Lumfur's lunch," I answered.

"Teamwork!" we said together, and gave each other our triple high five.

The Lumfur I had locked in the cage snorted, and Lamar and I jumped. Then the creature rolled over onto his side, tucked his head beneath his arm, and continued sleeping.

"Let's get out of here before any of his buddies return," whispered Lamar, which was exactly what I was thinking.

The circle of cages was surrounded by a thick wall of bushes that towered over our heads by at least one foot.

There was only one large gap in the leafy wall, so the way out (and, we hoped, the way back to the spaceship) was clear. But as we were about to leave, Lamar said, "Wait."

He looked back at the cages.

"Can I have that remote for a minute?"

"Sure," I said.

He took the remote and ran back to the three cages that held the rabbits. One by one he used the pattern to open the locks on cages 1, 3, and 8. As soon as the doors popped open, the rabbits scurried out of their prisons and disappeared into a small hole beneath the bushy wall.

"They probably didn't like being caged any more than we did," said Lamar.

We hurried out through the large gap and down a path that led away from the sleeping Lumfur and the empty cages. The bushes were soon replaced by trees. Not trees like the one with square leaves next to Fooz's spaceship, but turquoise-colored trees shaped like inverted cones, balancing on their points. Their wide leafy upper branches acted like umbrellas, blocking most of the sunlight. After the heat of being out in the open, the cool shade of the trees was a welcome change.

Bright purple birds zigzagged over our heads, singing three-note songs back and forth to each other. The sides of the path were lined with hundreds of red and yellow flowers. And the air no longer reeked like the Lumfurs, but instead smelled like equal parts peppermints, popcorn, and licorice. I began to relax, just a fraction. A small fraction, like $\frac{1}{16}$ th.

I was about to point out to Lamar that the number of petals on the red flowers were all multiples of 3 and the

40

number of petals on the yellow flowers were all multiples of 4 when he said, "I wonder how far it is to the spaceship."

We had both been inside a bag when we were carried to the cages, so neither of us saw how far we had traveled. But that didn't stop us from figuring out an answer.

"The Lumfur took 1,986 steps while I was riding on his back," I said.

"And I bet each of his steps was about a yard long," said Lamar.

That was all we needed to calculate how far we had gone.

I rounded 1,986 to 2,000, then multiplied by 3, the number of feet in one yard.

"That's about 6,000 feet," I said.

"And a mile is 5,280 feet," said Lamar, "so we're a little farther than a mile from the spaceship. We're both in good shape. If we walk at a speed of four miles per hour, I bet we can be at the ship in about fifteen minutes."

"*If* you can keep up with me," I said, and started jogging.

"You mean if *you* can keep up with *me*!" said Lamar, passing me with a challenging look.

But we both came to a sudden stop a few minutes later when the path split in two. We caught our breaths and studied both paths.

"What do you think?" asked Lamar. "Left or right?"

I like to think I'm good at noticing details, but as hard as I tried, the two paths looked the same.

Finally I said, "Maybe we should ask Lincoln."

Lincoln was Lamar's lucky penny. He had found it just before we won last year's Math All-Stars citywide tournament. It was minted in the year we both had been born, which we thought was a good sign.

Lamar took the penny from his back pocket. "Heads we go left, tails we go right. We've got a fifty-fifty chance of going the right direction. If it's wrong, we can backtrack and try the other path." He flipped the coin and caught it with one hand, then slapped it onto the back of the other.

"Tails."

We headed down the path to the right, but we hadn't gone very far before that path split again. Lamar flipped the penny a second time, and this time we went left.

Within five minutes the path had split four more times.

"This is crazy," said Lamar. "If each of the paths that we didn't choose also split into two, then after six divisions, that's . . ."

We worked the math out in our heads.

"Sixty-four different paths!"

Even Lincoln's luck couldn't hold out for that long.

"In other words . . ." I said.

"Yup," said Lamar. "We're lost."

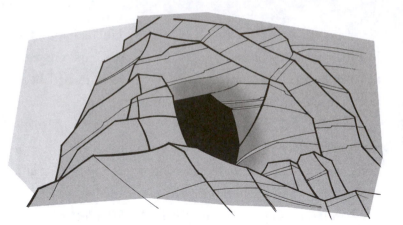

CHAPTER 2 + 2 + 2

Down the Rabbit Hole

Lamar suggested climbing a tree to look for the spaceship, but when we tried to do that, the branches of the cone-shaped trees were as rubbery as wet noodles. They wouldn't hold our weight, and we didn't get a foot off the ground.

I suggested hollering for help, hoping that Fooz's audio beam would pick up our voices. Then I realized the Lumfurs would hear us too, and neither Lamar nor I wanted to meet up with one of those furry monsters again.

"We could start a signal fire," said Lamar.

"Or we could keep going and hope for the best," I said.

"Or you could simply follow me," said a quiet voice from behind us.

We spun around. A lime-green rabbit with three long ears was watching us, twitching his six whiskers. It looked exactly like one of the rabbits Lamar had freed, except a third larger.

"Follow you *where*?" asked Lamar. By now, something as weird as a talking green rabbit didn't seem weird at all.

The rabbit didn't answer. Instead he began hopping down the path to the right.

Lamar and I exchanged glances.

"Do you have any better ideas?" asked Lamar.

"I don't," I said. "Let's go!"

The two of us took off.

Both Lamar and I are good runners, but we were already tired and it was all we could do to keep up. Right, left, left, right, left, right. I tried to remember which paths the rabbit chose in case this turned out to be a trap and we needed to retrace our steps, but I couldn't recognize a pattern and soon lost track of where we were going.

Just when I didn't think I could run another meter, the rabbit stopped in front of a hole in the side of a rocky cliff. He glanced over his shoulder then bounded inside the dark opening.

Lamar and I stood with our hands on our knees, panting. Too winded to even speak, we just nodded our heads at each other. Lamar climbed in first, then I followed.

The diameter of the hole was about the width of a school desk. I had to crawl on my hands and knees to fit inside. Soon it was so dark I couldn't see Lamar only a few inches in front of me. I began to wonder if following this strange rabbit was such a good idea after all.

After a few feet the tunnel began to slope downward at a forty-five-degree angle. I kept sliding into Lamar's tennis shoes until—*thud!*—the tunnel emptied us out into a large cavern.

The walls of the cavern were covered with crystal triangular prisms, glowing like thirty-watt light bulbs. Scattered around the sides of the cavern were thirty tunnels leading in all different directions. It was easy to tell exactly how many there were because they were all numbered. In the center of the cavern was a trio of three-eared rabbits, sitting at a three-legged table on tall three-legged stools. One rabbit was lime green, one rabbit was yellow, and one rabbit was orange. Each wore a crown of three braided vines, and each held a silver trident in its paw.

"Here they are, your highnesses," said the rabbit we had followed.

"Thank you, Greeley," said the green rabbit on the stool. "You are dismissed."

Greeley bowed low and hopped into tunnel 7.

The three rabbits at the table turned to look at us.

"We have brought you here to thank you for saving three members of our families," said the green rabbit.

"We are very grateful," continued the yellow rabbit, "and we would like to repay you for your kindness."

"Hmph!" snorted the orange rabbit, not looking very grateful at all.

"You're welcome," said Lamar. "We were glad to help. And as a matter of fact, you *could* do something for us. We're lost and we need to get back to our friend's spaceship."

"It's located next to a large pool of fludge," I added.

"Is that all?" said the green rabbit. "No sooner said than done."

"It's the least we can do," said the yellow rabbit.

The orange rabbit just glared.

"You are free to use any of our tunnels," said the green rabbit, spreading her arms wide. "And the way to your spaceship is easy. Simply follow the tunnel that is *not* an even number, and . . ." she turned to look at the yellow rabbit.

"And is *not* a multiple of 3, and . . ." both rabbits turned to the orange rabbit.

"And nothing!" sputtered the orange rabbit. "I refuse to give directions to these outsiders. They should not even be in our royal chambers." He scowled at the other rabbits. "As the two of you know, no other species may use our tunnel system unless the rulers of all three families are in agreement, and I most certainly do *not* agree."

"But they saved the lives of our kin," protested the green rabbit.

"They saved *your* kin," said the orange rabbit. "They saved no one from *my* family."

What a selfish creature, I thought, and from the look on Lamar's face I could tell he felt the same way. The other two rabbits looked embarrassed, but all they said was, "It *is* a rule. We *do* need to be in agreement."

"Get out!" shouted the orange rabbit, pointing his trident at the way we had entered.

I didn't like being ordered about by an animal that looked like it belonged in an Easter basket, but Lamar said,

"Fine! We don't want to use your rotten tunnels anyway. C'mon, Lexie, we'll find our way back to the spaceship on our own."

He turned to leave, but I said, "Wait. How about if we give you *this*?"

I held out the remote we had taken from the Lumfur.

"If a member of *any* of your families gets captured, you can use this to set them free."

I explained how the locks on the Lumfurs' cages worked, and the rabbits listened intently.

"Well . . ." said the orange rabbit, twitching his nose and staring at the remote. "Perhaps we can make a deal."

He jumped off his stool and hopped over to me, coming up only to my knees.

"You may use our tunnels in exchange for that box." He set down his trident and reached up with his tiny paws.

I held the remote behind my back.

"First tell us which tunnel leads to our spaceship," I said.

The rabbits nodded at each other and the green rabbit began again.

"The tunnel that you need is *not* an even number, and . . ."

"And is *not* a multiple of 3, and . . ."

"And is *not* a prime number," said the orange rabbit. "That is all you need to know."

"Thank you," I said, and handed him the Lumfur's remote. The other two rabbits clustered around him and began examining the box.

Meanwhile Lamar had taken a small notebook and a pencil stub from his pocket and had quickly written down the numbers from 1 to 30:

1 2 3 4 5 6 7 8 9 10 11 12 13 14 15
16 17 18 19 20 21 22 23 24 25 26 27 28 29 30

First he crossed off all the even numbers.

Then he crossed off all the multiples of 3.

Lamar's father had taught us about prime numbers years ago, so we knew that they were whole numbers greater than 1, and that they could only be divided evenly by themselves and the number 1. Lamar crossed off all of the primes.

There were only two numbers left.

"We came in through tunnel number 1," I said, "so the tunnel that we need is . . ."

"Twenty-five," said Lamar, circling it on his paper.

The rabbits were still whispering to one another as they examined the remote. They didn't even look up as we crawled into tunnel 25. The tunnel made one quick turn left then emptied us into a room the size of a very small closet.

My heart dropped. On the opposite wall were three more holes. If this tunnel kept dividing like the paths in the woods, we'd be just as lost as we were before.

"So which of these tunnels leads to our spaceship?" I said.

"They all do," said a familiar voice.

Poking his head through the tunnel we had just left was Greeley.

"The green rabbits use the first tunnel," he said, "the orange rabbits use the second tunnel, and the yellow rabbits use the third tunnel."

"We're in a hurry," said Lamar. "We want the shortest route."

Greeley frowned.

"I've only used the first tunnel," he said, "so I don't know which is the shortest. But each tunnel should be labeled with its length."

I looked a little closer and saw that above each opening, carved into the rock, was a tiny inscription.

Above the first tunnel was inscribed: 5 Grenkels.

Above the second tunnel was inscribed: 12 Orats.

And above the third tunnel was inscribed: 120 Yellens.

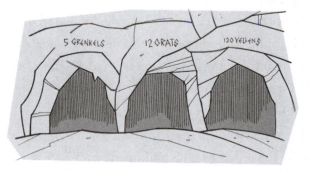

This wasn't very helpful at all.

"Don't all the rabbits use the same measuring system?" I asked.

"I'm afraid not," said Greeley. "Whenever we try to

convert our measurements to one system, there's a big argument over which one to use. It can be difficult for all three clans of rabbits to agree."

I had a pretty good guess about which rabbit would be the most disagreeable.

"So how long are a Grenkel, an Orat, and a Yellen?" asked Lamar.

"According to royal documents, one Grenkel equals six Orats," said Greeley. "And one Orat equals five Yellens."

"Greeley!" bellowed a voice from the throne room. "Come in here at once!"

"Excuse me," said Greeley. "I have to go." He disappeared, but a moment later his head popped back out from the tunnel. In a hushed voice he said, "No matter what King Crabby says, we're all very grateful for what you did. Especially me. One of the captives that you saved from the Lumfurs was my baby sister, Greta."

And with that, he was gone.

"Looks like we're on our own again," said Lamar.

He pulled out his pocket notebook once more and wrote the information that Greeley had given us:

1 Grenkel = 6 Orats

1 Orat = 5 Yellens

He glanced at the inscriptions above each opening, and when he looked at me, he had his Math All-Stars grin. He handed me a sheet of paper from his notebook and an extra pencil stub.

"I'll race you, Lexie. Let's see who can figure out which is the shortest tunnel first!"

CHAPTER 9,003

- <u>8,996</u>

Surrounded by Fludge

At first this problem looked complicated, but one thing I've learned is that a confusing math problem is often easier than it seems if I break it down into smaller parts.

I wanted to compare the lengths of these tunnels, but that was impossible if they were all in different units. First I had to convert the lengths to the same measuring system.

I started with the first two tunnels:

Tunnel 1 was 5 Grenkels long.

Tunnel 2 was 12 Orats long.

Then I drew a chart starting with the information from Greeley:

1 Grenkel = 6 Orats
 which meant
2 Grenkels = 12 Orats
3 Grenkels = 18 Orats
○ 4 Grenkels = 24 Orats
5 Grenkels = 30 Orats

Hooray! Two of the tunnels were now measured in the same units:

Tunnel 1 was 5 Grenkels or 30 Orats long.

And tunnel 2 was 12 Orats long.

I was halfway through solving this problem!

The third tunnel was measured in Yellens, so I flipped my paper over and started another chart starting with the other fact Greeley had told us:

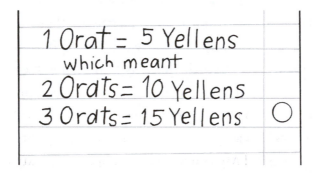

1 Orat = 5 Yellens
 which meant
2 Orats = 10 Yellens
3 Orats = 15 Yellens ○

I didn't need to continue with the chart. The pattern was pretty clear. If I wanted to change Orats into Yellens, all

I had to do was multiply by 5. That meant:

Tunnel 1 was 150 Yellens long (30 Orats × 5).

Tunnel 2 was 60 Yellens long (12 Orats × 5).

And I already knew that tunnel 3 was 120 Yellens long.

This problem wasn't that complicated after all! In fact, it was easy as 1, 2, 3, . . . or as easy as 150, 60, 120. The shortest tunnel was . . .

"Tunnel 2!" I told Lamar. "It's only 60 Yellens long."

Lamar was still scribbling on his paper. A few seconds later he looked up.

"You win, Lexie," he admitted. "At least *this* time. Tunnel 2 *is* the shortest. But I converted all three tunnels to Grenkels, and the way I figured it out, tunnel 2 is the shortest because it is only 2 Grenkels long."

No matter what measuring system we used, the second tunnel was definitely the shortest and was the route we wanted to take.

We climbed into the middle tunnel and began crawling. This time I took the lead. The floor was hard-packed dirt and it smelled damp and musty, like the basement in our apartment building. There weren't any glowing crystals here, so we were once again crawling in total darkness.

I was glad we had figured out the shortest route, but even though I knew this tunnel was only 60 Yellens long, that didn't mean a lot to me. How long was a Yellen? Was it the same length as a foot? A yard? It had better not be the length of a mile! My knees wouldn't hold up for sixty miles of crawling!

To pass the time as I crawled, and to take my mind off

how much my hands and knees were beginning to hurt, I began counting all the creatures we had met today: Fooz, Fluffy, Muffy, Puffy, the Lumfurs, Greeley, and all the three-eared rabbits. What a strange-looking group. On the other hand, I bet Lamar and I looked as strange to them as they did to us.

That's when I noticed that the tunnel was beginning to climb. I hoped that meant we were heading toward the surface. I also noticed that the sides of the tunnel were getting closer, as if we were crawling toward the small end of a funnel. Soon I had to squirm to keep moving. Maybe we were too big for this tunnel. Compared to the rabbits, we were more than triple their size.

"Oof!" I said, stopping suddenly. The tunnel had come to an abrupt end.

Lamar bumped into the back of my feet.

"Ouch!" he said. "What's wrong? Why did you stop?"

"It's a dead end," I replied.

This seemed odd. Greeley had told us that all three tunnels led to the spaceship.

"Maybe there's a door or a secret passage somewhere," said Lamar.

I certainly hoped so, because I didn't want to crawl *backward* all the way we had just come.

I began feeling around and discovered a smooth stone overhead. I pushed up, and the stone slid to one side.

Suddenly the tunnel was filled with fresh air and light. I squirmed my way out and Lamar did the same.

It took a full minute for our eyes to adjust to the

brightness. When they did, we saw that we had crawled out into some good news and some bad news.

The good news was that Fooz's spaceship was close by, just the length of a soccer field away.

The bad news was that we were on a tiny island in the middle of the giant lake of fludge.

We sat on the ground stretching our legs and arms as we looked around. After all that crawling, I thought my knees would be bent into right angles forever, but slowly they loosened up.

When we could stand again, I shielded my eyes with my hand and looked across the fludge. "Do you think Fooz can see us?"

"I don't know," said Lamar, "but maybe I can get her attention."

He picked up a flat round rock the size of a small pancake, took a step back, and threw it like a Frisbee toward the spaceship. It sailed about forty feet before landing in the lake. When it hit the fludge, it didn't splash, but sizzled. There was a small puff of grey smoke as the rock disintegrated.

"Looks like we're not swimming across," said Lamar.

When Fooz didn't appear, we realized we'd have to find a way to cross the fludge on our own. We began by inspecting the island.

It didn't take us long.

The shape of the island was a perfect circle, with a radius of only ten feet (give or take a few inches). And it was flat. No plants. No animals. Just hard-packed dirt scattered

with disc-shaped rocks. Some of the rocks were as small as pennies and some were as big as dinner plates. The opening leading to the tunnel was also perfectly round and in the exact middle of the island. There was nothing else, except for one thing . . .

Alongside the shore was a four-foot by four-foot square metal platform. On the floor of the platform was a rectangular plaque engraved with a message. We bent down to read it:

> To cross the lake
> Is simple indeed:
> Just read what's symmetrical,
> That's all that you need.

Beneath the poem were four strange words and a picture of a three-eared rabbit's face:

"That doesn't make any sense," I said.

I knew what symmetry meant. It's when you can divide a shape down the middle into identical parts. If you can't, then the shape isn't symmetrical, it's asymmetrical. The face of the rabbit was symmetrical. The circular island was symmetrical. The square platform was symmetrical. But the words didn't look symmetrical at all.

"How are we supposed to *read what's symmetrical*?" I asked.

"Maybe the letters are scrambled," said Lamar. "If we unscramble each of the four groups, maybe the message will make more sense."

We tried, but neither of us could find a way to turn the jumble of letters into words that we recognized.

Was there something else on the island that we were supposed to read? While Lamar kept studying the plaque, I walked the perimeter of the island, searching for anything we might have overlooked. All I found were rocks. Rocks, rocks, and more rocks. And even though I flipped at least 150 of them over, I didn't find anything else to read, symmetrical *or* asymmetrical.

Then I heard a low rumble. At first I thought it was an approaching thunderstorm, or worse, a Lumfur growling at us from the opposite shore. But the second time I heard it, I realized what the sound was. It was my stomach.

Lamar's stomach growled back.

Not only was I hungry, I was tired. Really tired. All I wanted to do now was go home, have a twelve-ounce glass of 2 percent milk, a half dozen of my dad's tacos, and climb into my twin-size bed with my king-size pillow. But I couldn't do any of that if we couldn't get off this island.

Were we going to be stuck here forever?

Not on your life! Not when we had both captains of the champion Math All-Stars team working on this problem. And as it turned out, everything we needed to get off the island was right there on that plaque.

CHAPTER 2³

Traveling in Reverse

"Lexie!" called Lamar. He was standing on the metallic platform looking down at the inscription. "I've got an idea."

I joined him at the edge of the plaque.

He pointed at the four strange words:

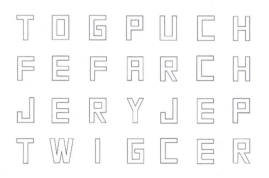

"The inscription is telling us we should *read what's symmetrical*," he said.

"I know," I said, "but the words *aren't* symmetrical."

"No, but the shape of some of the letters are. How about if we read the message using only the letters with symmetrical shapes?"

It was another excellent idea.

To help us keep track, I scooped up a handful of pebbles the size of nickels. We went through the message letter by letter, covering the letters that were asymmetrical with stones. The *T* and the *O* could easily be divided down the middle into identical halves, but the G and the *P* could not, so I covered each of them with a small rock. The *U* was symmetrical, but when I went to cover the letter *C*, Lamar said, "Look again."

He was right. When I looked at the *C* sideways, it was easy to see that it could be divided into identical halves too.

When we had finished covering all the asymmetrical letters, we were left with this message:

"You're brilliant!" I told Lamar. He smiled and gave a slight bow.

I placed my pointer finger on the engraving of the rabbit's face and gently pressed each eye two times.

Instantly there was a humming sound beneath us and the platform began to glide away from the shore. I stood up from my kneeling position, but when I did, the platform wobbled dangerously, so I quickly knelt back down again. Neither of us wanted to be dumped into the toxic waste so we remained as motionless as possible as the platform floated across the lake at a steady five miles per hour.

When it reached the shore, we both jumped off at the same time. We ran the remaining yards to Fooz's spaceship and hurried up the entrance ramp into the ship.

It was empty.

We looked through the hatch door in the floor, down into the fuel bay, but that was empty too.

Where was Fooz? Had she become worried and gone looking for us? Maybe she had been captured by the Lumfurs, too! How would we rescue her without the remote?

"I am sorry this has taken so long," said a high squeaky voice from over our heads. Fooz popped her head down from an opening in the spaceship's ceiling. "When we landed, one of my energy converters was damaged. But do not worry. I have now made all of the needed repairs and the ship is ready to leave."

She dropped to the floor of the cabin.

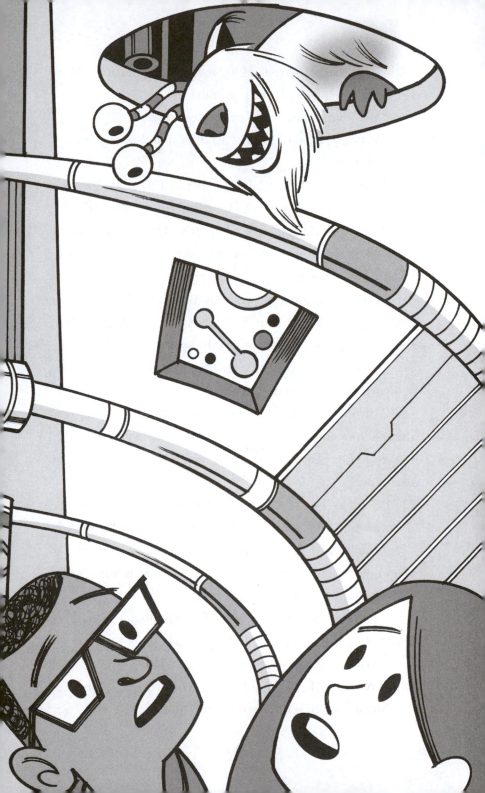

"I see that you are back from your explorations. Have you seen enough of planet Flacknar?"

"Yes!" we shouted. *More than enough.*

"Very good," said Fooz. "Strap yourself in and we will be on our way."

In less time than it takes to divide a number by itself, the engines were roaring and we lifted off the ground.

As we sped through space Lamar and I took turns telling Fooz what had happened to us while she was collecting fuel and making repairs to her ship. Her ping-pong-ball eyes darted back and forth between us as we explained how we had escaped from the Lumfurs' cages, navigated the rabbits' tunnels, and crossed the pool of fludge.

"Not only are you smarter than chickens," she told us, "you are nearly as smart as I am."

I'm not sure about Lamar, but I dozed off. The next thing I remembered was Fooz telling us, "We are within range of your planet. If you are ready, I am able to send you back now."

"Thanks, Fooz," said Lamar. "Without a doubt this was the craziest day of my life . . . but I'm glad that it happened."

"Me, too," I said. "Now if we can only find a way to keep our families from being angry. My dad is going to be furious that I'm coming home so late."

"And my parents have probably organized two dozen searching parties by now," added Lamar.

Fooz tilted her head to one side. "Late? Why do you have to be late? I can return you to your planet at any time that you would like."

66

"You can really do that?" asked Lamar.

"It is easy," said Fooz. "All you need to do is tell me how much time you would like me to reverse."

Lamar looked at me. "Let's go back to 4:00. That was the time on the clock in the lobby when we entered our apartment's elevator."

I had a better idea.

"No," I said. "Let's go back to 3:45. That's *before* we broke Mrs. Kruegel's jar of sun tea."

Lamar gave me an admiring look. "Smart thinking, Lexie. Now *you're* the brilliant one!"

I showed Lamar my watch. It was 4:09 a.m. No wonder we were so hungry and tired! If we wanted to go back to 3:45 p.m., how much time did Fooz need to reverse? Lamar and I made the computations in our heads, then compared our answers to see if we agreed.

We did.

"Send us back twelve hours and twenty-four minutes."

"Certainly, of course," said Fooz. "Please stand close together. And do not forget your egg." Lamar picked up his soccer ball and tucked it under his arm.

"After you send us back, are you going to try to capture a real chicken?" I asked.

Fooz stroked her furry face with one of her six legs. "I have been thinking about that. After getting to know the two of you, I do not feel the same way about locking strange animals inside cages anymore. Instead I will take a holographic video of a chicken. That will suffice for our zoo."

"Good luck," I said. "And thanks again!"

She padded to her control panel, stood on her back legs, and made adjustments to three dials. She smiled her toothy smile and said, "The coordinates are set. Good-bye, my friends."

Before we could say good-bye in return, she pressed a silver knob and there was another blinding flash of green light. My skin felt prickly like it was being poked with a hundred thousand toothbrush bristles. With the sound of crackling fireworks in my ear, I hoped that Fooz had all her coordinates correct. I didn't want to end up at the North Pole or in the middle of the Atlantic Ocean.

I didn't. Lamar and I were standing in front of our apartment building again.

"Look!" I said.

Mrs. Kruegel's jar of sun tea was sitting on the front steps, unbroken. This called for two sets of our triple high five.

I was glad that we wouldn't have to face Mrs. Kruegel after all, but when I thought about it, she no longer seemed so scary. After having dealt with the Lumfurs, I didn't think I'd ever be afraid of Mrs. Kruegel again.

Neither of us felt like kicking the soccer ball anymore, so we sat on the front stoop.

"There's one thing I can't figure out," I told Lamar. "If Fooz sent us back in time, does that mean none of those things on Planet Flacknar ever happened?"

Both our stomachs growled.

"I'm not sure," said Lamar. "But if they *didn't* happen, would our stomachs be as hungry as mine feels?"

We decided to go inside and find a snack. There was no way I could wait another ninety-five more minutes until my dad and I had dinner.

As Lamar pushed the button for the elevator, he asked, "So, do you think we'll ever see Fooz again?"

I thought about all the other places Fooz could be exploring. There were probably billions of other galaxies. Maybe even quadrillions. And each one of those could have a billion different planets to explore.

I shook my head sadly. "No, I don't think so. Not in 237 million years."

"Yeah, I suppose you're right," said Lamar.

But this time it turned out that my calculations were 100 percent wrong.

LAMAR'S NOTEBOOK
Feed the Blobs

Hey! This is Lamar. When Lexie and I got back to Earth, I decided to start this notebook to keep track of the weird things that happened on our trip. Especially the stuff about math. Math is definitely on my list of favorite things, along with soccer, my mom's triple chocolate fudge brownies, and sleeping late on Saturday. Who knows, someday I might be a famous mathematician like Archimedes or Benjamin Banneker. Or my dad. Well, my dad isn't actually famous. But he's a math professor at a university, and he's *very* smart.

One of the things I like about math is that there can be lots of ways to figure out a math problem. Once I solve a problem, sometimes I go back and see if I can get the same answer a different way. Okay, maybe that sounds a little weird, but like I said, I like math a lot.

For instance, take those blobs on Fooz's spaceship. Lexie and I figured out how many bogberries to feed them by making guesses and checking our answers. It's a good strategy, and it worked (just in time, too). But I thought of another way we could have figured out the answer. And the new way I found didn't involve any guessing.

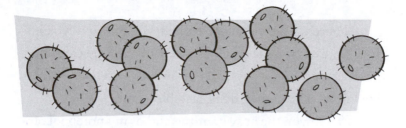

Suppose this fuzzball stands for the amount of food Muffy eats: *

Puffy would eat twice as much, or two fuzzballs: * *

Fluffy eats twice as much as that, or four fuzzballs: * * * *

Add them up. That's seven servings of food: * * * * * * *

We had thirty-five berries to divide up evenly among those seven servings: 35 divided by 7 equals 5. That means each one of those fuzzballs stands for five berries: 5 for Muffy, 10 for Puffy, and 20 for Fluffy. Pretty cool, huh? Same answer, but a completely different way to get it. And I didn't have to guess to figure it out.

After finding this new way to solve the problem, I was ready to take on another group of blobs. There weren't any hanging around our apartment building (Mrs. Kruegel would have had them evicted for being too slimy), so instead I made up a blob problem to give to the kids on our math team. See if *you* can figure it out. Use any strategy you want.

There were three blobs named Mo, Flo, and Kokomo Joe. Flo eats twice as much as Mo. Kokomo Joe eats *three times* as much as Flo. You've got seventy-two bogberries to feed them. How much does each blob get?

I'll tell you the answer at the end of my notebook. In the meantime, keep an eye out for blob tentacles! And if you solved my puzzle, try making up your own blob puzzle for a friend—but make sure you know the answer first. You don't want those blobs getting mad at you!

A Square Deal

Lexie thought she could fool me when she asked how many leaves were on the tenth branch of that tree next to Fooz's spaceship. I have to admit, I *was* stumped at first. There were way too many leaves to count. But I could tell that Lexie knew the answer, and if she had figured it out, then I was going to figure it out, too.

Do you know what gave me a clue? The shape of the leaves. They were square. That reminded me of square numbers. And that was the key to figuring out how many leaves were on each branch.

When you multiply a number by itself, you get a square number. $3 \times 3 = 9$, so 9 is a square number. You can see for yourself why they are called *square* numbers:

72

Take a sheet of grid paper. Draw a square on it. Your square can be any size, tiny or humungous. Just make sure that each side of your square is the same length. Next, count the number of smaller squares inside the square that you just drew. Your total will always be a square number.

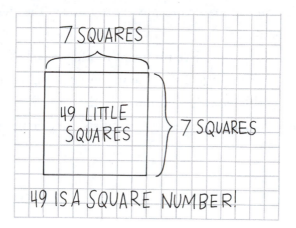

7 SQUARES

49 LITTLE SQUARES

7 SQUARES

49 IS A SQUARE NUMBER!

These are the first five square numbers:

1   (1 × 1)
4   (2 × 2)
9   (3 × 3)
16 (4 × 4)
25 (5 × 5)

When I started counting the number of leaves on the lower branches, I recognized the pattern right away. That made it simple to figure out how many leaves were on the tenth branch: 100 (10 × 10). Multiplying by 10 is always easy: just add a zero to the number that you are multiplying.

I even knew how many leaves were on the 100th branch of the tree: 10,000 (100 × 100). Multiplying by 100 is also easy: just add *two* zeroes to the number that you are multiplying.

That tree was pretty tall. If there were 1,000 branches, how many leaves do you think were on the 1,000th branch? If the pattern continued, I know the answer. Do you? You can compare your answer to mine at the end of my notebook.

You can write square numbers another way. It looks like this: 3^2. That little 2 floating in the air means multiply three by itself (3×3). The number in the air is called an exponent. Mathematicians and scientists use exponents all the time. So . . .

$3^2 = 9$

$4^2 = 16$

$5^2 = 25$

$6^2 = 36$

Pretty fancy, eh?

If we hadn't been captured by the Lumfurs, I would have started looking around to see if the planet had any trees with *cube*-shaped leaves. A cube is when you multiply a number by itself, and then multiply it by itself again.

$1 \times 1 \times 1 = 1$ 1 is a cube number

$2 \times 2 \times 2 = 8$ 8 is a cube number

$3 \times 3 \times 3 = 27$ 27 is a cube number

No surprise, but you can write cube numbers with exponents, too. Except this time, the exponent would be a little floating 3:

$1^3 = 1 \times 1 \times 1 = 1$

$2^3 = 2 \times 2 \times 2 = 8$

$3^3 = 3 \times 3 \times 3 = 27$

$4^3 = 4 \times 4 \times 4 = 64$

$5^3 = 5 \times 5 \times 5 = 125$

When you start using exponents, numbers can get big fast. And I mean BIG.

Ready to do some serious calculating? How many leaves would be on the 10th branch of a *cube* tree? That's 10^3, or $10 \times 10 \times 10$.

How about the 100th branch of a cube tree (100^3)?

Don't get freaked out by all these big numbers. Just remember how easy it is to multiply by 10 or 100. When you've got your answers, check them with mine and see if we agree.

Puzzling Patterns

Believe me, I was glad when we escaped from those stinky Lumfurs. Not only did they have disgusting eating habits, but they smelled like the Dumpster behind the cafeteria at school. Ugh!

But as gross as those creatures were, there was one thing I liked about them: the pattern that they used to unlock their numbered cages.

Patterns are cool. You can find them everywhere. In music. In nature. Even the design on my soccer ball makes a repeated pattern.

And lots of times finding a pattern can help solve a math problem. I spotted a pattern to help me figure out the number of leaves on the tenth branch of the square tree. Lexie told me she used a pattern to help her find which of the rabbits' tunnels was the shortest. And of course we needed to know the pattern so we could open the locks on the Lumfurs' cages.

As I said, patterns are cool. But watch out! They can also be tricky!

Here are the first three numbers of a pattern I made up. See if you can figure out what number comes next:

1, 2, 4, ?

Have you got your answer?

Did you say 8?

If you did, then I fooled you! But don't feel too bad. It looks like 8 should come next because the numbers seem to be doubling. But the next number in my pattern is actually 7.

It's easier to figure out a pattern when you have a lot of examples. I'll give you a few more numbers in my pattern, then see if you can figure it:

1, 2, 4, 7, 11, 16, 22, ?

If you're not sure, here's a clue. Think about how much each number increases as the pattern continues.

Did you get it? The next number is 29. I added 1 to the first number (1 + 1 = 2), I added 2 to the second number (2 + 2 = 4), I added 3 to the third number (4 + 3 = 7), and that was my pattern.

One of the most famous patterns in math is called the Fibonacci sequence. It was named after a guy who lived in Italy 800 years ago. My dad has several books about him, but my favorite is a book that I found at my school library, *Blockhead: The Life of Fibonacci*, by Joseph D'Agnese. Fibonacci loved numbers just as much as Lexie and I do. He traveled all over the world learning about math. When I get older, I'm going to have adventures like that, too!

Here's his famous number sequence:

1, 1, 2, 3, 5, 8, 13, 21, 34, ?

Can you figure out the pattern and what number comes next? Here's a clue: He also used adding to get the next number, but he used it in a different way than I did in my pattern.

To get this sequence, Fibonacci added the first two numbers (1 + 1) to get 2. Then he added the second and third numbers together (1 + 2) to get 3. He added the third and fourth numbers together (2 + 3) to get 5. Can you figure out the next number in his sequence after 34?

The weird (and cool) thing about the numbers in the Fibonacci sequence is that they pop up all the time in nature: the number of spirals on a pinecone, the number of petals on a flower. Like I said, patterns are everywhere.

I made up a few more patterns and tried to stump Lexie. See if you can find the next three numbers in each pattern. They start out easy, and then get harder:

#1: 0, 7, 14, 21, 28, 35, ___, ___, ___
#2: 201, 312, 423, 534, 645, ___, ___, ___
#3: 1, 4, 2, 5, 3, 6, 4, 7, ___, ___, ___
#4: 100, 98, 94, 88, 80, 70, 58, ___, ___, ___
#5: 3, 3, 5, 4, 4, 3, 5, ___, ___, ___

The last pattern is especially tricky. I even fooled my dad, and it's almost impossible to do that. I *almost* fooled Lexie. She had to think about it overnight, and she also needed this clue: compare the words *one*, *two*, *three*, *four*, *five*, *six*, *seven*, etc., to the corresponding numbers in the sequence. As I said, it's a tricky pattern.

Good luck! The answers are at the back of my notebook if you need them.

Taking Your Chances with Probability

When Lexie and I were lost in the woods, we turned to my lucky penny Lincoln for help. I know that he's not *really* lucky. If there are two choices and only one of them is correct, the chances of Lincoln picking the right choice are only 50 percent, or half the time. And with all those paths splitting into sixty-four different choices, the chances, or probability, of picking the one path that led to the spaceship was only 1 out of 64 . . . and that's not likely at all. It's a good thing Greeley came along and led us to the rabbits' cave.

Even though my lucky penny can't always tell us the right thing to do, I still like flipping Lincoln and thinking about probability. When I flip him, there are two possible outcomes: heads or tails. So the chances of him landing on heads are 1 out of 2. I can also write that as a fraction: ½. Or I can show it as a percentage: 50 percent. They all mean the same thing.

Instead of flipping a penny, if I roll a six-sided die, then my chances of rolling any one specific number would be 1 out of 6, or 1/6. There are six possible outcomes, and it's just as likely that any one of those numbers would come up.

But then I started thinking about rolling *two* dice. What would be the chances of rolling a specific number then? The lowest number I could roll with two dice would be a 2, and the highest number I could roll would be a 12. I could also roll any of the numbers in-between. That meant I could roll a 2, 3, 4, 5, 6, 7, 8, 9, 10, 11, or a 12. That's eleven different numbers. Did that mean the chances of me rolling any one of those specific numbers were equal, 1 out of 11?

That didn't seem right. I've played a lot of board games and I know that some numbers, like 12, are a lot harder to roll than other numbers. Why is that?

I decided to use math to figure it out.

First I made a chart with all the possible outcomes I could get from rolling two dice. I saw that there were 36 different ways that the dice could land.

Then I added up the totals for each of those thirty-six different combinations:

FIRST DIE	SECOND DIE	TOTAL		FIRST DIE	SECOND DIE	TOTAL		FIRST DIE	SECOND DIE	TOTAL
1	+ 1	= 2		2	+ 1	= 3		3	+ 1	= 4
1	+ 2	= 3		2	+ 2	= 4		3	+ 2	= 5
1	+ 3	= 4		2	+ 3	= 5		3	+ 3	= 6
1	+ 4	= 5		2	+ 4	= 6		3	+ 4	= 7
1	+ 5	= 6		2	+ 5	= 7		3	+ 5	= 8
1	+ 6	= 7		2	+ 6	= 8		3	+ 6	= 9

FIRST DIE	SECOND DIE	TOTAL		FIRST DIE	SECOND DIE	TOTAL		FIRST DIE	SECOND DIE	TOTAL
4	+ 1	= 5		5	+ 1	= 6		6	+ 1	= 7
4	+ 2	= 6		5	+ 2	= 7		6	+ 2	= 8
4	+ 3	= 7		5	+ 3	= 8		6	+ 3	= 9
4	+ 4	= 8		5	+ 4	= 9		6	+ 4	= 10
4	+ 5	= 9		5	+ 5	= 10		6	+ 5	= 11
4	+ 6	= 10		5	+ 6	= 11		6	+ 6	= 12

Finally I made a list showing how many ways there were to make each of those totals:

TOTAL OF THE TWO DICE	NUMBER OF DIFFERENT WAYS TO MAKE THAT TOTAL
2	1
3	2
4	3
5	4
6	5
7	6
8	5
9	4
10	3
11	2
12	1

Now it was easy to see why it was so hard to roll a 12 with two dice! There was just one combination (6 + 6) that equals 12. The chances of me rolling that combination were only 1 out of 36, or 1/36. Rolling a 2 with two dice was just as hard.

On the other hand, can you tell which number I would be the *most* likely to roll?

Yup. Number 7.

There are *six* different possible combinations that give me a total of 7. The chances of rolling that number are 6 out of 36, which is a lot more likely than 1 out of 36.

If you don't believe me, try it yourself:

Get two dice. Take a piece of paper and write the numbers 2 through 12 along one side (those are the different totals that you could roll with two dice).

Then start rolling dice. After each roll, put a tally mark next to the total that you rolled.

After ten rolls, which number has the most marks?

How about after twenty rolls? Fifty? One hundred? Get a friend to work with you, and I bet you could test 200 rolls in less than ten minutes. What does your chart look like then? Does it start to match up with the predicted probability of which numbers are the most likely to roll and which are the least likely?

Knowing about probability is handy if you like to play games, especially games that use dice or cards. I love games. I love making up games. And I love winning at games.

Possible totals with dice

2
3
4 |
5 ||
6
7 |
8 |||
9
10
11
12

Here's a game that I made up. You can try it yourself, and if you know about probability, it will help you to win!

First, draw a game board like mine. Don't worry if it isn't exactly the same shape or if it has a different number of spaces on the trail.

Second, color some of the spaces on the trail blue. Color the rest of them red.

Now you're ready to play!

You and your friend take turns rolling a six-sided die to move along the trail. BUT . . . before you roll, predict which color you'll land on. Roll the die, and if you land on the predicted color, you get to move an extra space.

Do you want to increase your chances of winning? Of course you do! Use what you know about probability. Before you make your prediction, count the colors on the next six spaces of the trail. For example, at the start of my game board, four of the first six spaces are blue and two of the first six spaces are red. Because you're rolling just one die, it's just as likely that you could roll any one of those six numbers. The chances of landing on a blue space are 4 out of 6, and the chances of landing on a red space are 2 out of 6. It's more likely that you'd land on a blue space, so that's what you should predict. Of course if three of the spaces are blue and three are red, your chances would be the same. You won't *always* be right about your predictions, but the chances are you'll be right more often than you'll be wrong . . . *if* you use probability.

Try making up a new game using three different colors on the trail. It will be harder to predict the right color now since there are three possible outcomes, but you can still use probability to help you make your prediction.

Here's one more probability puzzle. Suppose I flipped Lincoln forty-nine times and he landed on heads forty-nine times in a row (it's not *likely*, but it's *possible*). What is the probability that when I flipped him a fiftieth time, he would land on heads again?

You know where to find the answer . . . at the end of my notebook!

Measuring Up

I thought it was very weird, not to mention confusing, that each of the families of rabbits on Planet Flacknar had their own measuring system. Who would be crazy enough to do that?

Then I thought about Earth. People in some countries measure length using inches, feet, and yards, but people in other countries measure length using centimeters, meters, and kilometers—the metric system. Why didn't the world just use one system? It didn't make sense.

So I asked my dad.

He put down the stack of math tests he was correcting.

"Which of those two measuring systems do *you* think the world should use?" he asked.

My dad is smart, but he has the annoying habit of answering my question with a question of his own. I suppose that's because he's a teacher.

"Well, which measuring system do *most* countries use?" I asked.

"The metric system," he said. "Without a doubt. It's much easier to use. There are only a few countries that don't use it: the United States, Liberia, and Myanmar."

"Then the answer is easy," I said. "Everyone in the world should switch over to the metric system."

My dad's eyes glowed like they do when he's

asking a sneaky math question or he's setting me up for a trap in chess.

"Are you sure? Think how much money it would cost the United States to switch. Think of all the things that would have to be changed: road signs, measurements on clothing, even football fields use yards. And that's just the beginning. All the manufacturing machines that use inches or feet would need to be changed, too. Do you still think it would be a good idea?"

Leave it to my dad to make me think the obvious answer wasn't as simple as it sounds.

But the more I thought about it, the more I still thought everyone should switch to one system of measurement. Especially when I read online about a multimillion-dollar Mars satellite that burned up because the team of people who built the satellite used one measuring system and the team of people operating it used another.

I also knew my dad was right that the metric system is a *lot* easier to use.

Just compare the two systems:

1 meter = 100 centimeters

vs.

1 foot = 12 inches

If I want to convert from meters to centimeters in the metric system, all I have to do is multiply by 100. For example, my school bus is about 11 meters long. To convert that to centimeters, I multiply it by 100. My bus is 1,100 (11 × 100) centimeters long. I can figure out that answer in my head instantly.

On the other hand, my school bus is about 36 feet long. To change that to inches, I have to multiply by 12. I can do it, but even though I'm really good at math, it's not as easy. My bus is 432 (36 × 12) inches long.

All the units of length in the metric system are based on tens, hundreds, and thousands. That makes it easy to convert from one to the other.

1 centimeter = 10 millimeters

1 meter = 100 centimeters

1 kilometer = 1,000 meters

The other systems of measurement in the metric system (liters for measuring liquids and grams for measuring weight or mass) are also just as easy to use.

If I ever get back to Flacknar, maybe I can convince all the rabbits to use the metric system. Then I had another idea. Maybe I could invent a brand NEW measuring system!

I decided to give it a try.

For the basic unit of length in my measuring system I chose the height of my soccer ball. I marked it off on a straight piece of wood. I named this new unit after me: the Lamar.

I knew I would need to measure smaller units, so I divided the stick into five equal parts. I named each of those smaller parts after one of my goldfish: the Zip.

And then for measuring really long things, I decided 25 Lamars would equal 1 Banneker (Benjamin Banneker is my favorite mathematician). So . . .

1 Lamar = 5 Zips

1 Banneker = 25 Lamars

Then I used my new ruler to measure things.

My toothbrush was 4 Zips long.

My bed was 8 ½ Lamars long.

And the apartment hallway was 1 Banneker, 15 Lamars, and 2 Zips long!

Try it yourself. Make up your own measuring system:

* Decide on a your own basic unit of measurement.

* Mark it off on a straight stick or piece of cardboard.

* Divide it into equal smaller units.

* Give your new measuring units names.

Now start measure things in your house, apartment, or classroom.

Using your new measuring system, how long is your bed? A crayon? Your desk?

I still think everyone in the world should use just one measuring system. But even though it might not be very practical, it could be fun to have a secret measuring system that only you and your friend know about. Maybe Lexie and I will make up one together.

Simply Symmetry

It's a good thing we deciphered the rabbits' message out on that island, or we still might be surrounded by fludge.

Decoding the message was tricky, but I liked that

puzzle because it involved symmetrical shapes. Math isn't only about numbers.

Symmetry is something that even kindergarteners use. If you fold a piece of paper in half and cut away from the fold, the shape that you get is always symmetrical. It could be as simple as a heart (like the ones we used to make Mother's Day cards in kindergarten), or as complicated as this two-headed dino-bot:

Try it yourself. Fold a piece of paper in half, grab a pair of scissors, and see what wild, or simple, shape you can make (just be sure you don't cut away the entire folded edge or you will end up with two separate pieces). When you open up the paper, the shape will always be symmetrical.

The dividing line down the middle (along the fold) is the called the line of symmetry (I didn't learn that in kindergarten, but I learned it a couple of years later). Some symmetrical shapes have only one line of symmetry, like my dino-bot, but others have more. Sometimes a lot more.

Here's an equilateral triangle:

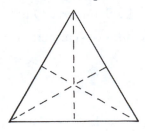

It's got three lines of symmetry. You could fold it in half along any of those dotted lines, and the two sides would match up perfectly.

A square has four lines of symmetry:

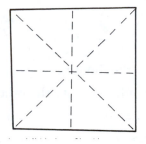

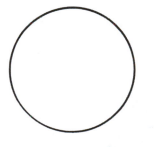

Can you guess how many lines of symmetry this circle has?

Give up?

An infinite amount! That's even more than Lexie can count.

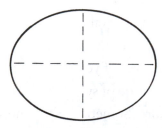

But if you stretch the circle out to make an oval:

Then it's got only two lines of symmetry.

Okay, it's time for Lamar's Sneaky Symmetry Quiz!

Can you first figure how many lines of symmetry each of these shapes has?

The more I thought about the message on the island, the more I wondered about the other letters of the alphabet. First I drew all the letters on a piece of paper, making them look like the letters we saw on the plaque.

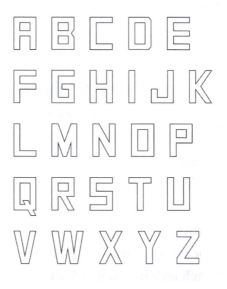

Then I started a list of which ones were symmetrical, and which ones were asymmetrical, or *not* symmetrical. At first it was pretty clear which category each letter fell into. Then I got to the letter *N*:

I couldn't fold it in half to make each side match up. On the other hand, if I divided it in the middle, each of the two halves were exactly the same shape, except one half was flipped the other direction. Was this shape symmetrical, or not?

I asked my dad again. But first he asked *me* a question (no surprise there). He wanted to know what *I* thought.

I told him that I thought the letter *N wasn't* symmetrical, because it couldn't be folded in half.

He said that I was right . . . and wrong. My dad is sneaky like that.

It turns out that there are two types of symmetry. Lateral or mirror symmetry is the kind of symmetry when one side is a reflection of the other side. It includes all the shapes you get when cutting a folded piece of paper in half.

And I was right. The letter *N* did *not* have lateral symmetry.

But he told me there's another type of symmetry called radial or rotational symmetry. That's when a shape can be turned, or rotated, around a central point. As it turns, it will match up with itself at least once before making a complete rotation. He told me the letter *N did* have rotational symmetry.

I wanted to prove it, so I cut the shape of the letter *N* out of paper. I stuck a pin in the very middle, then traced around the outside edge. I rotated the letter, and sure enough, it matched up with itself halfway through the rotation.

Snowflakes have rotational symmetry. So do starfish. And so does this weird creature that I drew:

You can't fold it equally in half, but if you rotate it once all the way around, it matches up with itself four times, so that means it has a rotational order of symmetry 4. (I found that online *without* asking my dad!)

I started a new chart. In one column I listed all the letters that had only lateral symmetry, like the letter *A*. In the second column I listed all the letters that had only rotational symmetry, like the letter *N*. In the third column I listed all the letters that had both lateral AND rotational symmetry, like the letter *X*. And in the fourth column I listed the letters that weren't symmetrical at all. They were asymmetrical, like the letter *F*. Can you predict which column had the most letters?

I wrote a message to Lexie and I told her that if she wanted to read it, she had to read only the symmetrical letters and numbers, whether they had lateral symmetry, rotational symmetry, or both.

I couldn't stump Lexie, but maybe I can stump you!

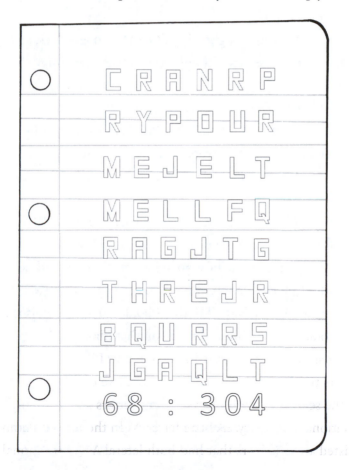

LAMAR'S NOTEBOOK – 7
Answers to Lamar's Puzzles

TOP SECRET!

Don't peek until you've tried to figure out the answers yourself!

Feed the Blobs

Mo eats 8 bogberries, Flo eats 16 bogberries, and Kokomo Joe eats 48 bogberries. That's one hungry blob!

A Square Deal

There would be 1,000,000 leaves on the 1,000th branch of a *square* tree. That's one million.

There would be 1,000 leaves on the 10th branch of a *cube* tree.

There would be 1,000,000 leaves on the 100th branch of a *cube* tree. That's a million, too.

Just imagine how many leaves there would be on the 1,000th branch of a *cube* tree. That's 1,000 × 1,000 × 1,000, or $1,000^3$. That's 1,000,000,000, which is the same as one billion. I told you that numbers can get big when you start using exponents!

Puzzling Patterns

The next number in Fibonacci's sequence after 34 is 55 (21 + 34).

And here are the answers to *my* patterns:

#1: 0, 7, 14, 21, 28, 35, <u>42</u>, <u>49</u>, <u>56</u>
(The pattern is counting by 7's.)

#2: 201, 312, 423, 534, 645, <u>756</u>, <u>867</u>, <u>978</u>
(Each digit in the number increases by 1.)

#3: 1, 4, 2, 5, 3, 6, 4, 7, <u>5</u>, <u>8</u>, <u>6</u>
(First I added 3, then I subtracted 2)

#4: 100, 98, 94, 88, 80, 70, 58, <u>44</u>, <u>28</u>, <u>10</u>
(First I subtracted 2, then I subtracted 4, then I subtracted 6, then I subtracted 8, etc.)

#5: 3, 3, 5, 4, 4, 3, 5, <u>5</u>, <u>4</u>, <u>3</u>
(These are the number of letters in the words *one*, *two*, *three*, *four*, *five*, *six*, *seven*, etc. The next three numbers would be 5, 4, 3, the number of letters in the words *eight*, *nine*, and *ten*. I warned you this last pattern was tricky!)

Taking Your Chances with Probability

It doesn't matter what has happened in the past, the chances of Lincoln landing on heads stay the same: 1 out of 2, or 50 percent. And just so you know, I've flipped Lincoln a lot of times, and he's *never* come up heads 50 times in a row!

Simply Symmetry

Here are the answers to my symmetry quiz:

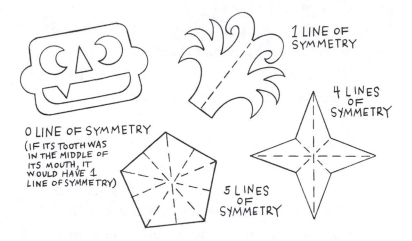

When I sorted out the letters, twelve had only lateral symmetry: *A, B, C, D, E, K, M, T, U, V, W, Y*

Three had only rotational symmetry: *N, S, Z.*

Four had lateral AND rotational symmetry: *H, I, O, X.*

Seven were asymmetrical: *F, G, J, L, P, Q, R.*

And here's the secret message I wrote to Lexie:

CAN

YOU

MEET

ME

AT

THE

BUS

AT

8:30